Goldilocks
and the
Three Bears

Adapted by Amanda Askew
Illustrated by Bruno Merz

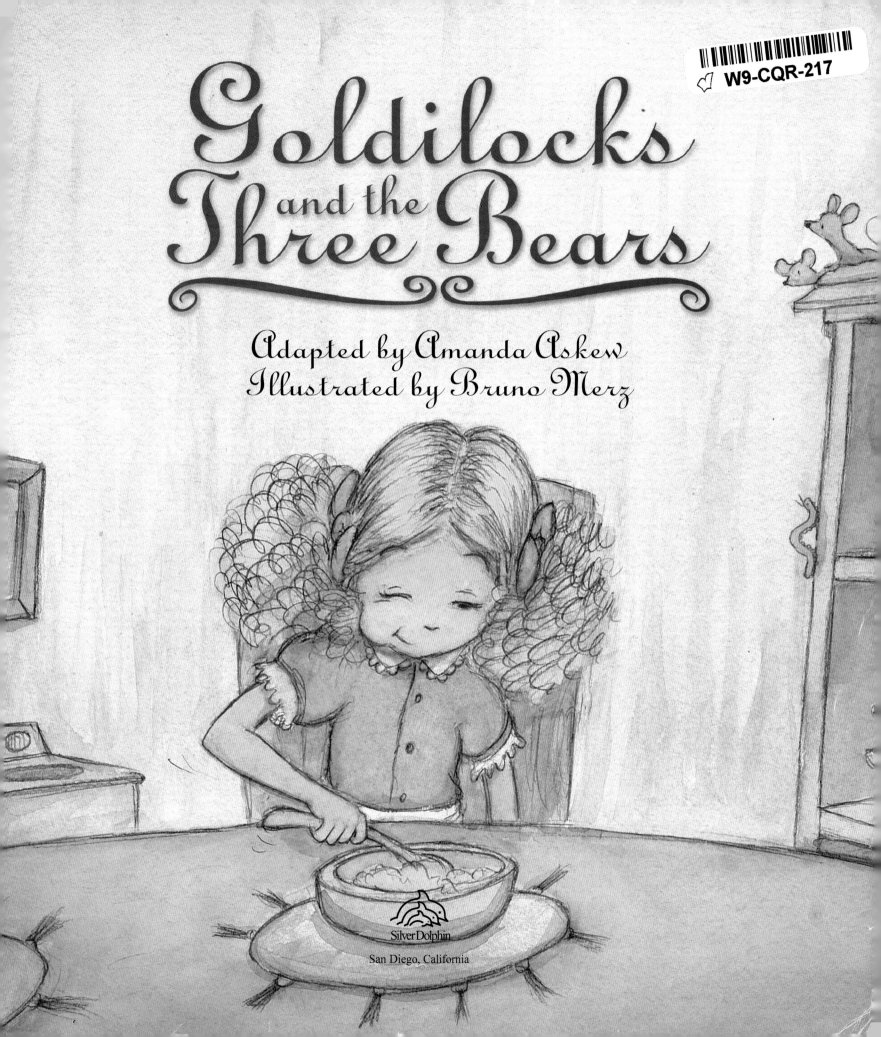

Silver Dolphin

San Diego, California

One day, a little girl called Goldilocks went for a walk in the forest.

She came upon a house and knocked on the door. When no one answered, Goldilocks went inside.

At the table in the kitchen, there were three
bowls of porridge. Goldilocks was hungry.

She tasted the porridge in the first bowl.

"This porridge is too hot!" she exclaimed.

Then she tasted the porridge in the second bowl.

"This porridge is too cold!" she cried.

Finally, she tasted the last bowl of porridge.

"Ahh, this porridge is just right," she said. And with that, she ate it all up.

After she'd eaten the porridge,
Goldilocks went into the living
room, where she saw three chairs.

She started to feel a little tired.

Goldilocks sat in the first chair to rest her feet.

"This chair is too hard!" she exclaimed.

Then she sat in the second chair.

"This chair is too big!" she whined.

Finally, she tried the last and smallest chair.

"Ahhh, this chair is just right," she sighed.

Just as she settled down into the chair
to rest, it broke into pieces.

Goldilocks wanted to lie down, so she decided to try the bedroom.

She lay down on the first bed, but it was too hard.

Then she lay down on the second bed, but it was too soft.

Last, she lay down on the third bed, and it was just right.

Goldilocks fell asleep.

As she was sleeping, the three bears who lived in the cottage came home. They went into the kitchen, and what did they see?

"Someone's been eating my porridge," growled Papa Bear.

"Someone's been eating my porridge," said Mama Bear.

"Someone's been eating my porridge, and they've eaten it all up!" cried Baby Bear.

Next, the three bears went into the living room, and what did they see?

"Someone's been sitting in my chair," growled Papa Bear.

"Someone's been sitting in my chair," said Mama Bear.

"Someone's been sitting in my chair, and they've broken it to pieces," cried Baby Bear.

The three bears began to look around, and when they got to the bedroom, what did they see?

"Someone's been sleeping in my bed," growled Papa Bear.

"Someone's been sleeping in my bed,"
said Mama Bear.

"Someone's been sleeping in
my bed, and she's still there!"
cried Baby Bear.

Just then, Goldilocks woke up and saw the three bears.
The bears didn't look very happy.

"Help!" Goldilocks screamed.

She jumped up and ran out of the room.

Goldilocks ran out the door and into
the forest. Never again did she go
wandering in the forest near the home
of the three bears.

Notes for parents and teachers

- Look at the front cover of the book together. Can the children guess what the story might be about? Read the title together. Does this give them more of a clue?

- When the children first read the story, or you read it together, can they guess what might happen at the end?

- What do the children think of the characters? Is Goldilocks kind? What about the three bears? Who is their favorite character, and why?

- The three bears are a family of animals who act like humans. Can the children think of any other stories with similar characters?

- When the bears get home, do the children think they will find Goldilocks? What do the children think the bears should have done to Goldilocks?

- The bears eat porridge. Do the children know what porridge is? What do they like to eat? Where would they eat their favorite meal? Ask the children to draw or paint their ideal eating experience.

- What other endings can the children think of? Ask the children to act out the story, and then the new endings.

- By eating the bears' porridge and breaking the chair, Goldilocks acts selfishly. What other acts can the children think of that are selfish?

Silver Dolphin Books
An imprint of the Baker & Taylor Publishing Group
10350 Barnes Canyon Road, San Diego, CA 92121
SilverDolphin www.silverdolphinbooks.com

Copyright © QEB Publishing, Inc. 2010

ISBN-13: 978-1-60710-352-3
ISBN-10: 1-60710-352-4

Manufactured, printed, and assembled in Guangdong, China.
1 2 3 4 5 15 14 13 12 11

The Library of Congress has cataloged the original QEB edition as follows:

Askew, Amanda.
  Goldilocks and the three bears / as told by Amanda Askew.
    p. cm. -- (QEB storytime classics)
  Summary: Lost in the woods, a tired and hungry little girl finds the house of the three bears where she helps herself to food and goes to sleep.
  ISBN 978-1-59566-792-2 (library binding)
  [1. Folklore 2. Bears--Folklore.] I. Goldilocks and the three bears.
English. II. Title.
  PZ8.1.A776Go 2010
  398.2--dc22
  [E]
                                        2010005385

Editor: Amanda Askew
Designers: Vida and Luke Kelly